Knock yourself out!

237½ sidesplitting, totally ridiculous, not always original, hilarious, a little bit stupid...jokes, quotes, and really dumb sayings

By someone you'd never want to sit next to!

Compiled by Wynn Wheldon

MQP

Published by MQ Publications Limited
12 The Ivories, 6-8 Northampton Street, London N1 2HY
Tel: 020 7359 2244 Fax: 020 7359 1616
email: mail@mqpublications.com
website: www.mqpublications.com

Copyright © MQ Publications Limited 2004

Text compiled by: Wynn Wheldon

ISBN: 1-84072-634-2

Printed and bound in China

The purpose of this book is to make you giggle.

Researching it made me giggle. Ideally it ought to make others giggle, too. Read it out to your nearest and dearest. Read it out to your enemies. And giggle as you do so, because funnier than any joke is laughter itself. In 1962 in Tanganyika there was an outbreak of contagious laughing among schoolgirls that lasted six months. The schools had to be closed.

For laughter can be a serious business, a matter sometimes of life and death: "Verrius witnessed that Zeuxis, the very excellent portraitist, died from laughing ceaselessly over the grimace of an old lady that he himself had painted," wrote Laurent Joubert, a concerned Frenchman of the sixteenth century.

Not everybody laughs at the same thing. One of my sisters, who generally laughs loudly and generously, hasn't much time for comedians, especially on television; my wife is an avid viewer of "Frasier" but can live without "Seinfeld;" my mother hated P.G. Wodehouse, but loved Dickens; the first time I saw my father cry he was watching Jacques Tati in Jour de Fête. My sons think Mr. Bean is hilarious. I think my sons are hilarious.

"Anything awful makes me laugh," wrote Charles Lamb. In the pages to follow you will find pictures of people freed from all kinds of burden, existing in the blessed timeless moment that laughter creates. The words that accompany them should also crease a face or two, thereby minutely raising the nation's need for Botox.

Should you be of a reflective temperament and not easily moved to uncontrollable amusement or foolish levity or, indeed, Botox, Robert Benchley's rules for laughing may be helpful (or not): "In order to laugh at something, it is necessary (1) to know what you are laughing at, (2) to know why you are laughing, (3) to ask some people why they think you are laughing, (4) to jot down a few notes, (5) to laugh. Even then, the thing may not be cleared up for days."

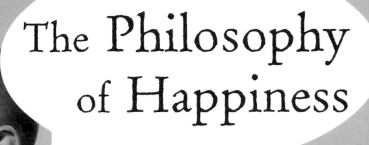

The Philosophy
of Happiness

CHAPTER 1

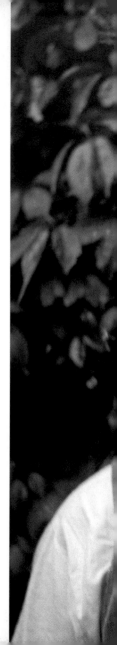

Always try to keep a smile on your face—it looks silly anywhere else.

In order to laugh at something, it is necessary (1) to know what you are laughing at, (2) to know why you are laughing, (3) to ask some people why they think you are laughing, (4) to jot down a few notes, (5) to laugh. Even then, the thing may not be cleared up for days.

ROBERT BENCHLEY

You can pretend to be serious;
you can't pretend to be witty.

SACHA GUITRY

**Start every day with a smile
and get it over with.**

W.C. FIELDS

Humor, a good sense of it, is to Americans what manhood is to Spaniards and we will go to great lengths to prove it. Experiments with laboratory rats have shown that, if one psychologist in the room laughs at something a rat does, all of the other psychologists in the room will laugh equally.

GARRISON KEILLOR

Even if there is nothing to laugh about, laugh on credit.

He who laughs last
has not yet heard
the bad news.

BERTOLT BRECHT

**If you're going to tell people
the truth, make them laugh,
or they'll kill you.**

Billy Wilder

When a person can no longer laugh at himself, it is time for others to laugh at him.

Thomas Szasz

I am thankful for laughter, except when milk comes out of my nose.

WOODY ALLEN

We do have a zeal for laughter in most situations, give or take a dentist.

JOSEPH HELLER

Those are my principles. If you don't like them I have others.

GROUCHO MARX

Frenchmen have a
peculiar sense of humor;
Americans find this out
when they try to talk to
them in French.

If you don't learn to laugh
at trouble, you won't have
anything to laugh at when
you're old.

ED HOWE

Laughter is the sensation of feeling good all over and showing it principally in one place.

JOSH BILLINGS

Man is the only animal that laughs, but when you look at some people, it's hard to understand how the animals keep from laughing.

Blessed are they who can laugh at themselves for they shall never cease to be amused.

Happiness is having a large, loving, caring, close-knit family in another city.

GEORGE BURNS

He who laughs
last, thinks
slowest.

He spoke with a certain what-is-it in his voice, and I could see that, if not actually disgruntled, he was far from being gruntled.

P.G. WODEHOUSE

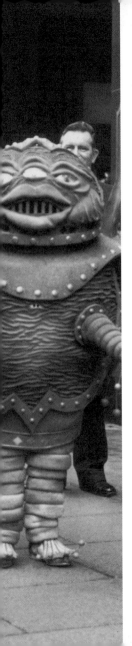

Do not take life too seriously. You will never get out of it alive.

ELBERT HUBBARD

Seven days without laughter makes one weak.

MORT WALKER

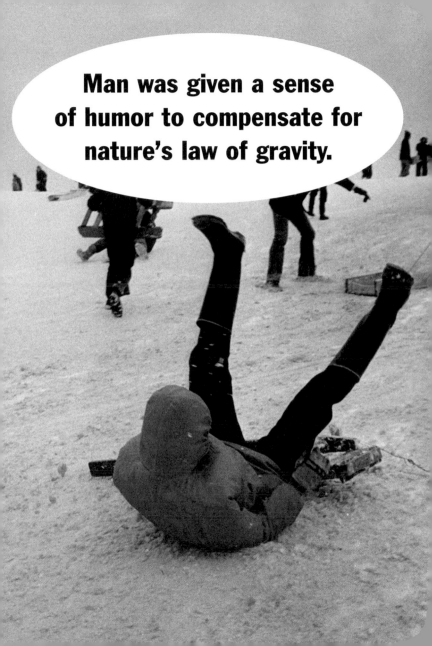

**Those who can't laugh
at themselves leave
the job to others.**

Laugh and the whole
world laughs with you,
cry and...you have to
blow your nose.

That's Folks for Ya!

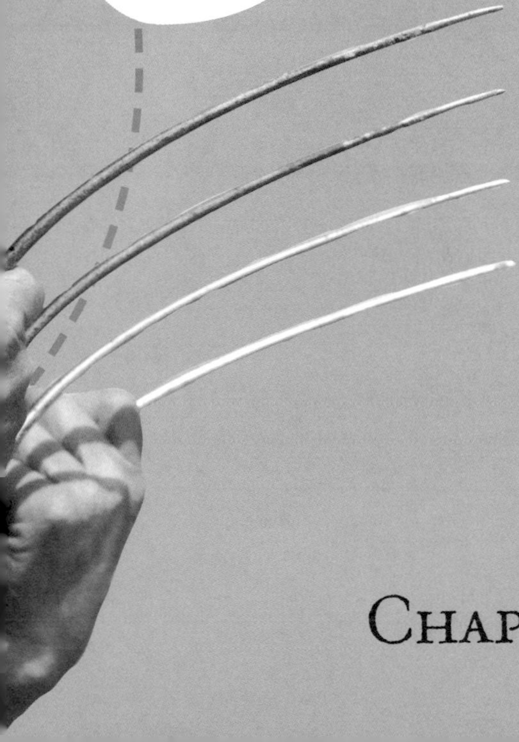

CHAPTER 2

Does she have something on her mind?

Only if she's got a hat on.

Anyone who says he
can see through women
is missing a lot.

GROUCHO MARX

Women want to find one man to satisfy their many needs, while men want many women to satisfy their one need.

ANKA RADAKOVICH

That's the first mistake we've made since that guy sold us the Brooklyn Bridge.

Stan Laurel

A gossip is one who talks to you about others; a bore is one who talks to you about himself; and a brilliant conversationalist is one who talks to you about yourself.

Lisa Kirk

There are two ways to handle a woman, and nobody knows either of them.

KIN HUBBARD

What is it that even the most careful person overlooks?

Her nose.

Two tourists are driving through Louisiana. They're coming up to a town called Natchitoches. They start arguing about how you pronounce the name of the town. They keep arguing until they stop for lunch. Now they're at the counter, and one tourist asks the blonde employee, "Before we order, could you please settle an argument for us? Would you please pronounce where we are, very slowly?" The blonde girl leans across the counter and says, "Burrrrrrr-gerrrrrrrr Kiiiiiiing."

A minister was preoccupied with thoughts of how he was going to ask the congregation to come up with more money than they were expecting for repairs to the church building. Therefore, he was annoyed to find that the regular organist was sick and a substitute had been brought in at the last minute. The substitute wanted to know what to play. "Here's a copy of the service," the minister said impatiently. "But you'll have to think of something to play after I make the announcement about the finances." During the service, the minister paused and said, "Brothers and Sisters, we are in great difficulty; the roof repairs cost twice as much as we expected, and we need four thousand dollars more. Any of you who can pledge one hundred dollars, please stand up." At that moment, the substitute organist played The Star Spangled Banner.

I believe in equality for everyone, except reporters and photographers.

MAHATMA GANDHI

Real diamonds!
They must be worth
their weight in gold.

MARILYN MONROE

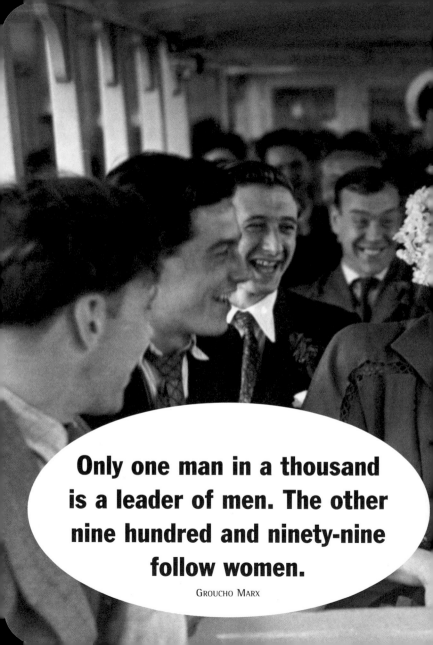

**Artificial intelligence
is no match for
natural stupidity.**

**Never argue with a fool.
People might not know
the difference.**

We must believe in luck.
For how else can we explain
the success of those we
don't like?

JEAN COCTEAU

Some people say that I must be a horrible person, but that's not true. I have the heart of a young boy— in a jar on my desk.

STEPHEN KING

I was walking home one night and a guy hammering on a roof called me a paranoid weirdo in morse code.

EMO PHILIPS

Clothes make the man. Naked people have little or no influence in society.

MARK TWAIN

An egotist is a person of low taste—more interested in himself than in me.

AMBROSE BIERCE

**If I were two-faced, would
I be wearing this one?**

ABRAHAM LINCOLN

Once a man indulges himself
in murder, very soon he comes
to think little of robbing, and
from robbing he comes next to
drinking and Sabbath-breaking,
and from that to incivility and
procrastination.

THOMAS DE QUINCEY

Animal
Antics

I wonder if other dogs think that poodles are members of a weird religious cult.

RITA RUDNER

No animal should ever jump up on the dining room furniture, unless absolutely certain that he can hold his own in conversation.

FRAN LEBOWITZ

I could dance with you till the cows come home. Better still, I'll dance with the cows till you come home.

Groucho Marx

Dogs feel very strongly that they should always go with you in the car, in case the need should arise for them to bark violently at nothing right in your ear.

Dave Barry

Why did the psychic chicken cross the road?

To get in touch with the other side.

It is not by accident that man is the only animal who has a sense of humor. He is also the only animal who wears clothing, denies himself sex, worships non-existent deities, starves in order to create, kills and dies for his country, slaves and cheats for his bank balance. Clearly, he is the only animal who NEEDS a sense of humor.

HARVEY MINDESS

Three turtles, Joe, Steve, and Poncho, decide to go on a picnic. Joe packs the picnic basket with cookies, bottled sodas, and sandwiches. The trouble is, the picnic site is 10 miles away, so the turtles take 10 whole days to get there. By the time they do arrive, everyone's whipped and hungry. Joe takes the stuff out of the basket, one by one. He takes out the sodas and realizes that they forgot to bring a bottle-opener. Joe and Steve beg Poncho to turn back home and retrieve it, but Poncho flatly refuses, knowing that they'll have eaten everything by the time he gets back.

Somehow, after about two hours, the turtles manage to convince Poncho to go, swearing on their great grandturtles' graves that they won't touch the food.

So, Poncho sets off down the road, slow and steady. Twenty days pass, but no Poncho. Joe and Steve are hungry and puzzled, but a promise is a promise. Another day passes, and still no Poncho, but a promise is a promise. After three more days have passed without Poncho in sight, Steve starts getting restless.

"I NEED FOOD!" he says with a hint of dementia in his voice.

"NO!" Joe retorts. "We promised."

Five more days pass. Joe realizes that Poncho probably skipped out to the Burger King down the road, so the two turtles weakly lift the lid, get a sandwich, and open their mouths to eat. But then, right at that instant, Poncho pops out from behind a rock.

"Just for that, I'm not going."

Why don't sheep shrink when it rains?

GEORGE CARLIN

A man was walking down the street with 20 penguins following him. A policeman came along and said, "What do you think you're doing? Take these animals to the zoo!" The next day, the policeman again saw the man walking with 20 penguins. "I thought I told you to take the penguins to the zoo yesterday?" he said. The man replied, "I did. We had such a good time, today we're going to the beach!"

Once upon a time, a beautiful princess happened upon a frog in a pond. The frog said to the princess, "I am a handsome prince but an evil witch has put a spell on me. One kiss from you and I will turn back into a prince and then we can marry, move into the castle with my mother and you can prepare my meals, clean my clothes, bear my children, and forever feel happy doing so." That night, while the princess dined on frog legs, she kept laughing and saying, "I don't think so."

Outside of a dog, books are a man's best friend; inside of a dog it's too dark to read.

GROUCHO MARX

How do elephants dive into swimming pools?

Head first.

Why do ducks have webbed feet?
To stamp out fires.

Why do elephants have flat feet?
To stamp out burning ducks.

A turtle was walking down an alley in New York when he was mugged by a gang of snails. A police detective came to investigate and asked the turtle if he could explain what happened. The turtle looked at the detective with a confused look on his face and replied: "I don't know, it all happened so fast."

**At today's pork prices,
being called a pig is
more of a compliment
than an insult.**

If there were any justice
in this world, people
would occasionally be
permitted to fly
over pigeons.

GENE BROWN

A black cat crossing your path signifies that the animal is going somewhere.

GROUCHO MARX

Montmorency [the dog] came and sat on things just when they were wanted to be packed. He put his leg into the jam, and he worried the teaspoons, and he pretended the lemons were rats, and got into the hamper and killed three of them.

JEROME K. JEROME

A boy can learn a lot from a dog: obedience, loyalty, and the importance of turning around three times before lying down.

ROBERT BENCHLEY

I spilled spot remover on my dog. Now he's gone.

STEVEN WRIGHT

All at Sea

CHAPTER 4

**Another advantage
of a nudist camp
is that you don't
have to sit around
for hours in a wet
bathing suit after
swimming.**

**How do you keep a
man from drowning?**

**Take your foot off
his head!**

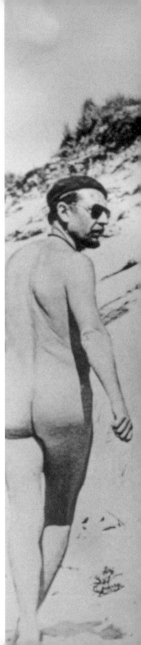

STREETS FULL OF WATER. PLEASE ADVISE.
(Telegram sent on arriving in Venice)

ROBERT BENCHLEY

My mother said she learned how to swim when someone took her out in the lake and threw her off the boat. I said, "They weren't trying to teach you how to swim."

PAULA POUNDSTONE

A preacher was completing a temperance sermon: with great expression he said, "If I had all the beer in the world, I'd take it and throw it into the river." With even greater emphasis he said, "And if I had all the wine in the world, I'd take it and throw it into the river." And then finally, he said, "And if I had all the whiskey in the world, I'd take it and throw it into the river." He sat down. The song leader then stood very cautiously and announced, "For our closing song, let us sing hymn number 365: 'Shall We Gather at the River.'"

The First Mate was in a rare mood as he finished drilling the crew. He barked out a final order: "All right, you idiots, fall out!" The men fell out, but one sailor stood firm. The sailor stared at the First Mate and smiled. "There were a lot of them, weren't there sir?"

A sure cure for seasickness is to sit under a tree.

SPIKE MILLIGAN

A fisherman was bragging about a monster of a fish he caught. A friend broke in and chided, "Yeah, I saw a picture of that fish and he was all of six inches long." "Yeah," said the proud fisherman, "but after battling for three hours, a fish can lose a lot of weight."

Sunburned and upset, Sandy returned to the office on Monday morning. "What's wrong Sandy?" asked one of her co-workers. "I've had it!" exclaimed Sandy; "I'm going on a diet once and for all!" "Oh you don't look so bad," said the co-worker. "Oh really?" pouted Sandy. "Sunday, I decided to go to the beach and fell asleep. I woke up with four men from Greenpeace pulling on my arms and legs and one was shouting: 'Quick, let's see if we can slide it back into the water!'"

Is ditchwater dull? Naturalists
with microscopes have told me
that it teems with quiet fun.

G.K. CHESTERTON

There's no use in
walking five miles
to fish when you can
depend on being just as
unsuccessful near home.

MARK TWAIN

The sailor walked into the galley and poured himself a cup of coffee. As he sipped it, he looked out the porthole and said "It looks like rain." Upset, the cook yelled at the sailor, "For the last time, it's coffee!"

The formula for water is H_2O. Is the formula for an ice cube H_2O squared?

LILY TOMLIN

I discovered I scream the same way whether I'm about to be devoured by a Great White or if a piece of seaweed touches my foot.

AXL ROSE

I knew a cannibal who had been influenced by Catholic missionaries. On Fridays he only ate fishermen.

TOMMY COOPER

Hope is a wonderful thing—one little nibble keeps a man fishing all day.

Since three-quarters of the earth's surface is water and one-fourth land, it's perfectly clear the good Lord intended that man spend three times as much time fishing as he does plowing.

How To Avoid Shark Attacks:

1. Never leave Kansas.
2. Roll in manure before diving. Sharks hate anything breaded.
3. Always dive with a buddy. On shark's approach, point to buddy.
4. Dive with a briefcase. Sharks may mistake you for an attorney and leave you alone out of professional courtesy.

"What is it that hangs on the wall, is green, wet, and whistles?"

I knitted my brow and thought and thought, and in final perplexity gave up.

"A herring," said my father.

"A herring?" I echoed. "A herring doesn't hang on the wall!"

"So hang it there."

"But a herring isn't green!" I protested.

"Paint it."

"But a herring isn't wet."

"If it's just painted it's still wet."

"But..." I sputtered, summoning all my outrage, "...a herring doesn't whistle!"

"Right," smiled my father. "I just put that in to make it hard."

LEO ROSTEN

If one morning I walked on top of the water across the Potomac River, the headline that afternoon would read: PRESIDENT CAN'T SWIM.

LYNDON B. JOHNSON

An angler is a man who sits around on riverbanks doing nothing because his wife won't let him sit around doing nothing at home.

IRISH TIMES

There's a fine line between fishing and standing on the shore looking like an idiot.

STEVEN WRIGHT

Why does the ocean roar?

You'd roar too, if you had that many crabs on your bottom.

REDD FOXX

How can you tell if a monster has a glass eye?

When it comes out in conversation.

It was the couple's first cruise and the husband was less than excited about their economy size cabin. Picking up the phone and dialing he said, "Is this room service?" "Yes," came the answer from the other end. "Good," said the husband, "send me up a room!"

Fishing is just about the most fun you can have with a worm on a string.

The Coast Guard cutter tuned in to a faint distress signal from a sinking pleasure craft. "What is your position? Repeat, what is your position?" shouted the radio operator into the microphone. Finally a faint reply crackled over the static: "I'm executive vice president of First Global Bank—please hurry!"

The Family

CHAPTER 5

You can learn many things from children. How much patience you have for instance.

FRANKLIN P. JONES

I want my children to have all the things I couldn't afford. Then I want to move in with them.

PHYLLIS DILLER

My mother buried three husbands...and two of them were only napping.

RITA RUDNER

Familiarity breeds contempt—and children.

MARK TWAIN

The reason grandchildren and grandparents get along so well is because they have a common enemy.

I'm going home next week.
It's a kind of emergency—
my parents are coming here.

RITA RUDNER

The highlight of my childhood was making my brother laugh so hard the food came out of his nose.

GARRISON KEILLOR

A lazy schoolboy lets his father do his homework, but a bright one helps his father with it.

A woman got on a bus holding a baby. The bus driver looked at the child and blurted out, "That's the ugliest baby I've ever seen!" Infuriated, the woman slammed her fare into the fare box and took an aisle seat near the rear of the bus. The man seated next to her sensed that she was agitated and asked her what was wrong. "The bus driver insulted me," she fumed. The man sympathized and said, "Why, he shouldn't say things to insult passengers. He could be fired for that." "You're right," she said. "I think I'll go back up there and give him a piece of my mind!" "That's a good idea," the man said. "Here, let me hold your monkey."

Martin had just received his brand new driver's license. The family troops out to the driveway, and climbs in the car, where he is going to take them for a ride for the first time. Dad immediately heads for the back seat, directly behind the newly minted driver. "I'll bet you're back there to get a change of scenery after all those months of sitting in the front passenger seat teaching me how to drive," says the beaming boy to his father. "Nope," comes Dad's reply, "I'm gonna sit here and kick the back of your seat, just like you've been doing to me all these years."

One day my father took me aside and left me there.

JACKIE VERNON

Teacher: "If you had one dollar and you asked your father for another, how many dollars would you have?"

Boy: "One dollar."

Teacher: "You don't know your arithmetic."

Boy: "You don't know my father."

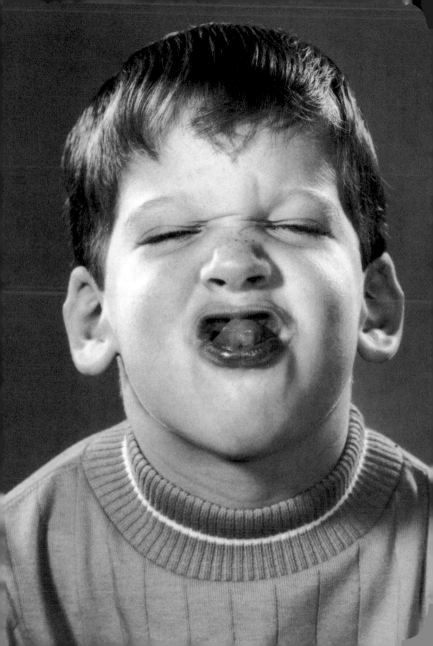

Any astronomer can predict with absolute accuracy just where every star in the universe will be at 11:30 tonight. He can make no such prediction about his teenage daughter.

JAMES T. ADAMS

Maybe there is no actual place called hell. Maybe hell is just having to listen to our grandparents breathe through their noses when they're eating sandwiches.

JIM CARREY

One of life's greatest mysteries is how the boy who wasn't good enough to marry your daughter can be the father of the smartest grandchild in the world.

You have to stay in shape. My grandmother, she started walking five miles a day when she was 60. She's 97 today and we don't know where the hell she is.

ELLEN DeGENERES

A young man asked an old rich man how he made his money. The old man fingered his worsted wool vest and said, "Well, son, it was 1932, the depth of the Great Depression. I was down to my last nickel. I invested that nickel in an apple. I spent the entire day polishing the apple and, at the end of the day, I sold the apple for ten cents.

The next morning, I invested those ten cents in two apples. I spent the entire day polishing them and sold them at 5:00pm for 20 cents. I continued this system for a month, by the end of which I'd accumulated a fortune of $1.37." The young man listened, rapt. The old man went on: "Then my wife's father died and left us two million dollars."

God gave us our relatives; thank God we can choose our friends.

ETHEL WATTS MUMFORD

My sister just had a baby. I can't wait to find out if I'm an aunt or an uncle.

GRACIE ALLEN

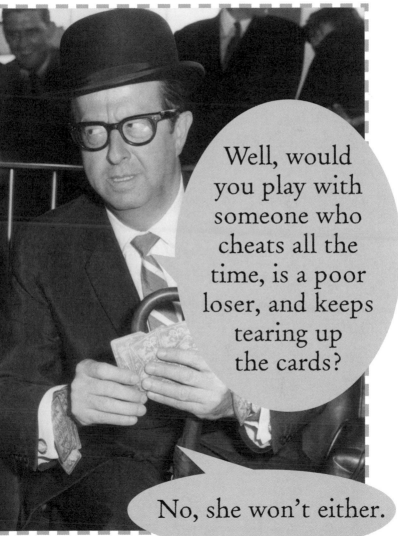

A lady and her daughter were in the theater. A strained voice called out through the darkened auditorium, "Please, is there a doctor in the house?" Several men stood up as the lights came on. The lady pulled her daughter to stand next to her, "Good, are any of you doctors single and interested in a date with a nice, Jewish girl?"

My aunt, she's had a terrible time. First off she got tonsillitis, followed by appendicitis and pneumonia. After that she got rheumatism, and to cap it off they gave her hypodermics and inoculations. I thought she would never get through that spelling bee.

JUDY CANOVA

Childhood is that wonderful time of life when all you need to do to lose weight is to take a bath.

RICHARD S. ZERA

Fatherhood
is pretending
the present
you love most is
soap-on-a-rope.

BILL COSBY

The quickest way for
a parent to get a child's
attention is to sit down
and look comfortable.

LANE OLINGHOUSE

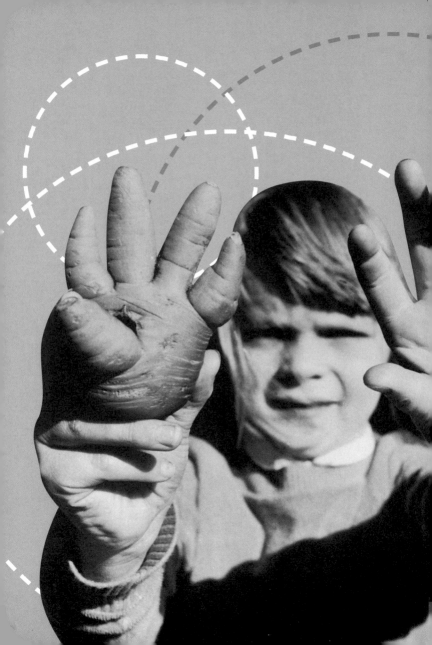

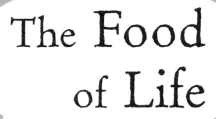

The Food of Life

CHAPTER 6

Tell the cook of this restaurant with my compliments that these are the very worst sandwiches in the whole world, and that when I ask for a watercress sandwich I do not mean a loaf with a field in the middle of it.

OSCAR WILDE

I am not a glutton—I am an explorer of food.

ERMA BOMBECK

A dietician was once addressing a large audience in Chicago. "The material we put into our stomachs is enough to have killed most of us sitting here, years ago. Red meat is awful. Vegetables can be disastrous, and none of us realizes the germs in our drinking water. But there is one thing that is the most dangerous of all and we all of us eat it. Can anyone here tell me what lethal product I'm referring to? You, sir, in the first row, please give us your idea." The man lowered his head and said, "Wedding cake."

Cucumber should be well sliced, dressed with pepper and vinegar, and then thrown out.

Samuel Johnson

Just about the time your income reaches the point where food prices don't matter—calories do.

An onion can make people cry, but there has never been a vegetable invented to make them laugh.

WILL ROGERS

A highbrow is the kind of person who looks at a sausage and thinks of Picasso.

A.P. HERBERT

...the British cook is a foolish woman who should be turned, for her iniquities, into a pillar of that salt which she never knows how to use...

OSCAR WILDE

Food prices are so high that it's no longer possible to bite off more than you can chew.

Watermelon—it's a good fruit. You eat, you drink, you wash your face.

ENRICO CARUSO

No one goes
to that restaurant
anymore—it's
too crowded.

A man walks into a doctor's office. He has a cucumber up his nose, a carrot in his left ear, and a banana in his right. "What's the matter with me?" he asks the doctor. The doctor replies, "You're not eating properly."

If you've got melted chocolate all over your hands, you're eating it too slowly.

A nice box of chocolates can provide your total daily intake of calories in one place.

**Into these bowls
Mrs Squeers poured
a brown composition
which looked like
diluted pincushions
without the covers.**

CHARLES DICKENS

To duplicate the taste
of hammerhead shark,
boil old newspapers
in Sloan's Liniment.

SPIKE MILLIGAN

They may be drinkers, Robin, but they're still human beings.

BATMAN

Eat at this restaurant and you'll never eat anywhere else again!

BOB PHILLIPS

Child training is a matter of teaching your child to eat his food instead of wearing it.

Cheese: milk's leap toward immortality.

CLIFTON FADIMAN

Coffee in England always tastes like a chemistry experiment.

AGATHA CHRISTIE

Chocolate has many preservatives. Preservatives make you look younger.

Artichokes…are just plain annoying….After all the trouble you go to, you get about as much actual "food" out of eating an artichoke as you would by licking thirty or forty postage stamps. Have the shrimp cocktail instead.

MISS PIGGY

Getting from A to B

CHAPTER 7

**Time, tide,
and bus drivers
wait for no man.**

Someone sent me a
postcard picture of the earth.
On the back it said, "Wish
you were here."

STEVEN WRIGHT

Thanks to the Interstate highway system, it is now possible to travel from coast to coast without seeing anything.

CHARLES KURALT

Have you ever noticed? Anybody going slower than you is an idiot, and anyone going faster than you is a maniac.

GEORGE CARLIN

I drove my car up to a toll booth. The man said, "Fifty cents." I said, "Sold."

SLAPPY WHITE

A Texas farmer visited Arizona and remarked how much he liked its blue skies and wide open spaces. Arizona reminded him of his home state. During his visit he wanted to see how Arizona's ranches compared to the large spreads they have in Texas. Driving down the highway, he saw a farmer on his tractor out in a field. The Texan stopped and hailed the farmer down. "Nice farm you have here," the Texan drawled. The farmer tipped his straw hat and politely said, "Thank you, sir." "How many acres do you farm?" the Texan asked. The Chino Valley farmer replied proudly, "2000 acres of alfalfa and 3500 acres of sweetcorn." The Texan smirked and said, "Pardner, on my ranch back home I get up every day at sun-up, get in my pickup, and by the time the sun sets I still haven't reached the end of my spread." The Arizona farmer replied, "Fella, I know just what you're talkin' about. I owned a pickup like that too a few years back."

Some guy hit my fender the other day, and I said unto him, "Be fruitful, and multiply." But not in those words.

WOODY ALLEN

When you're safe at home you wish you were having an adventure; when you're having an adventure you wish you were safe at home.

THORNTON WILDER

If the Lord had wanted people to fly, He would have made it simpler for people to get to the airport.

MILTON BERLE

When everything
is coming your way,
you're in the wrong lane.

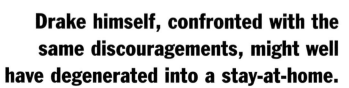

Drake himself, confronted with the same discouragements, might well have degenerated into a stay-at-home.

A.P. HERBERT (ON THE DIFFICULTIES OF PASSPORT REGULATIONS)

A man gets on the train with his son and gives the conductor one ticket. "How old's your kid?" asks the conductor, and the father says, "He's four years old." "He looks at least twelve to me," says the conductor, and the father says, "Can I help it if he worries?"

ROBERT BENCHLEY

Never lend your car to anyone to whom you have given birth.

ERMA BOMBECK

When a cat is dropped, it always lands on its feet, and when toast is dropped, it always lands with the buttered side facing down. If you strap buttered toast to the back of a cat, the two will hover, spinning inches above the ground. With a giant buttered-cat array, a high-speed monorail could easily link New York with Chicago.

If you look like your passport photo, you're too ill to travel.

WILL KOMMEN

If at first you don't succeed— so much for skydiving.

HENRY YOUNGMAN

OK, so what's the speed of dark?

STEVEN WRIGHT

There are two classes of travel—first class, and with children.

<small>Robert Benchley</small>

The sooner you fall behind, the more time you'll have to catch up.

<small>Steven Wright</small>

Bicycles are almost as good as guitars for meeting girls.

BOB WEIR

I was pulled over for speeding today. The officer said, "Don't you know the speed limit is 50mph?" I replied, "Yes, but I wasn't going to be out that long."

STEVEN WRIGHT

The most common of all antagonisms arises from a man's taking a seat beside you on the train, a seat to which he is completely entitled.

ROBERT BENCHLEY

That's Life

CHAPTER 8

One of the hardest
decisions in life is when
to start middle age.

HERBERT V. PROCHNOW AND HERBERT V. PROCHNOW JR

Life, you know, is
rather like opening
a tin of sardines. We
are all of us looking
for the key.

ALAN BENNETT

**If their IQs were
5 points lower, they
would be geraniums.**

RUSS FRANCIS

**Every once in a while
I feel I am at two with
the universe.**

WOODY ALLEN

Gordon died. So Susan went to the local paper to put a notice in the obituaries. The man at the counter, after offering his condolences, asked Susan what she would like to say about Gordon. "Just put, 'Gordon died,'" she said. The gentleman, somewhat perplexed, asked, "That's it? Just 'Gordon died?'"

Surely, there must be something more you'd like to say about Gordon. If it's money you're concerned about, the first five words are free. We really should say something more." So Susan pondered for a few minutes and finally said, "OK, then. You put, 'Gordon died. Yacht for sale.'"

Well, we can't stand around here doing nothing, people will think we're workmen.
SPIKE MILLIGAN

I like work; it fascinates me. I can sit and look at it for hours. I love to keep it by me; the idea of getting rid of it nearly breaks my heart.

JEROME K. JEROME

I have everything now I had twenty years ago—except now it's all lower.

GYPSY ROSE LEE

If everything is under control, you are going too slow.

MARIO ANDRETTI

Most women are attracted to the simple things in life. Like men.

Henry Youngman

At my age I do what Mark Twain did. I get my daily paper, look at the obituaries page and if I'm not there I carry on as usual.

PATRICK MOORE

The trouble with being punctual is that nobody's there to appreciate it.

FRANKLIN P. JONES

How long was I in the army?
Five foot eleven.

SPIKE MILLIGAN

I was decorated for saving
the lives of the entire regiment.

What did you do?

I shot the cook.

If thine enemy offend thee, give his child a drum.

CHINESE CURSE

241

Too bad the only people who know how to run the country are busy driving cabs and cutting hair.

GEORGE BURNS

It is better to have a permanent income than to be fascinating.

OSCAR WILDE

Have you ever had one of those days when you have had to murder a loved one because he is the devil?

EMO PHILIPS

When choosing between two evils, I always like to try the one I've never tried before.

MAE WEST

The strong young man at the construction site was bragging he could outdo anyone in a feat of strength. He made a special case of making fun of one of the older workmen. After several minutes, the older worker had had enough. "Why don't you put your money where your mouth is?" he said. "I will bet a week's wages that I can haul something in a wheelbarrow over to that outbuilding that you won't be able to wheel back." "You're on, old man," the braggart replied. "Let's see what you got." At that, the old man reached out and grabbed the wheelbarrow by the handles. Then, nodding to the young man, he said, "All right. Get in."

An executive is someone who can take three hours for lunch without hindering production.

I don't know what
effect the men will
have upon the enemy,
but, by God,
they terrify me.

DUKE OF WELLINGTON

In an unfortunate error we were made to say last week that the retiring Mr. South was a member of the defective branch of the local police force. Of course, this should have read "the detective branch of the local police farce."

CHRISTCHURCH STAR

According to a recent survey, men say the first thing they notice about women is their eyes. And women say the first thing they notice about men is they're a bunch of liars.

JAY LENO

You know you're getting
old when the candles cost
more than the cake.

BOB HOPE

**Life is what happens to
you while you're working
for your future.**

If falling in love is anything like learning how to spell, I don't want to do it. It takes too long.

GLENN, AGE 7

It may be that your sole purpose in life is simply to serve as a warning to others.

You can't have everything.
Where would you put it?

STEVEN WRIGHT

**There cannot
be a crisis next
week. My schedule
is already full.**

DR. HENRY KISSINGER

I have an existential map;
it has "you are here"
written all over it.

STEVEN WRIGHT

The Feel-Good Factor

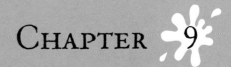

CHAPTER 9

**Be careful about reading
health books. You may
die of a misprint.**

MARK TWAIN

**All the things I really like
are either immoral, illegal,
or fattening.**

ALEXANDER WOOLLCOTT

I do not participate in any sport with ambulances at the bottom of a hill.

ERMA BOMBECK

Whenever I feel like exercise, I lie down until the feeling passes.

ROBERT M. HUTCHINS

If I'd known I was going to live this long, I'd have taken better care of myself.

Eubie Blake

I have the body of an eighteen year old. I keep it in the fridge.

Spike Milligan

Skiing: a winter sport that people learn in several sittings.

I still say a church steeple with a lightning rod on top shows a lack of confidence.

Doug McLeod

We met Dr Hall in such very deep mourning that either his mother, his wife, or himself must be dead.

Jane Austen

Sherlock Holmes and Dr. Watson go on a camping trip. After a good dinner and a bottle of wine, they retire for the night. Some hours later, Holmes wakes up and nudges his faithful friend. "Watson, look up at the sky and tell me what you see." "I see millions and millions of stars, Holmes," replies Watson. "And what do you deduce from that?" Watson ponders for a minute: "Well, astronomically, it tells me that there are millions of galaxies and potentially billions of planets. Astrologically, I observe that Saturn is in Leo. Horologically, I deduce that the time is approximately a quarter past three. Meteorologically, I suspect that we will have a beautiful day tomorrow. Theologically, I can see that God is all powerful, and that we are a small and insignificant part of the universe. What does it tell you, Holmes?" Holmes is silent for a moment. "Watson, you idiot!" he says. "Someone has stolen our tent!"

Was it murder—or something serious?

DICK POWELL

Either he's dead or my watch has stopped.

GROUCHO MARX

To me, boxing is like a ballet,
except there's no music,
no choreography and the
dancers hit each other.

JACK HANDY

**I saw the play under
adverse conditions—
the curtain was up.**

ROBERT BENCHLEY

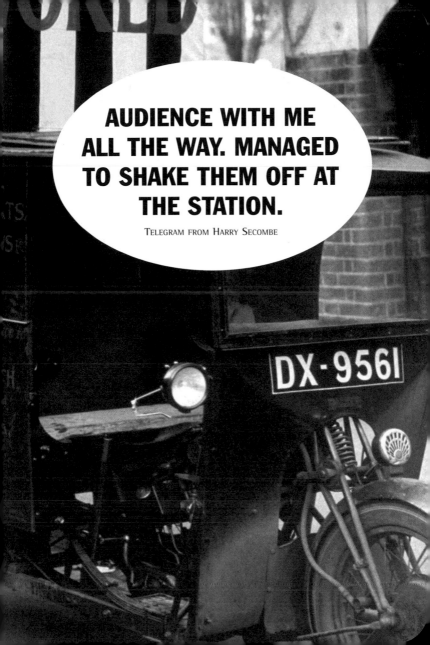

AUDIENCE WITH ME ALL THE WAY. MANAGED TO SHAKE THEM OFF AT THE STATION.

Telegram from Harry Secombe

I failed to make the chess team because of my height.

WOODY ALLEN

A recent study shows that 75 percent of the body's heat escapes through the head. I guess that means you could ski naked if you had a good hat.

JERRY SEINFELD

The only reason I would take up jogging is so that I could hear heavy breathing again.

ERMA BOMBECK

The only way to keep your health is to eat what you don't want, drink what you don't like, and do what you'd rather not.

MARK TWAIN

Everywhere is within walking distance if you have the time.

STEVEN WRIGHT

Quit worrying about your
health. It'll go away.

ROBERT ORBEN

**Early to rise and early to
bed makes a man healthy
and wealthy and dead.**

JAMES THURBER

**Anyone who goes to
a psychiatrist ought to
have his head examined.**

SAMUEL GOLDWYN

We didn't lose the game;
we just ran out of time.

VINCE LOMBARDI

To feel "fit as a fiddle" you must tone down your middle.

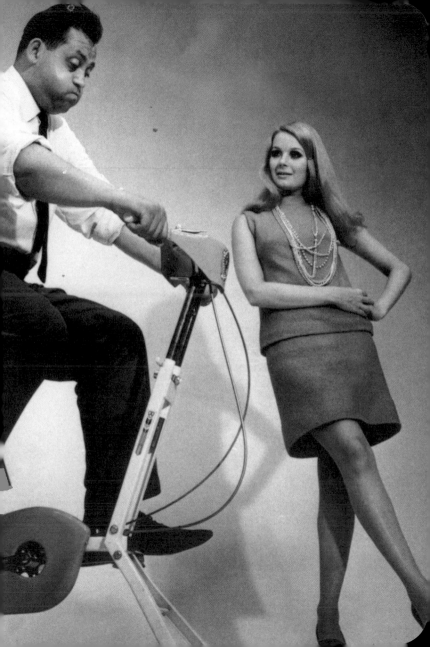

This guy has muscles in places where I don't even have places.

BOB HOPE

I'm in shape.
Round is a shape.

GEORGE CARLIN

Whoever thought up the word "Mammogram?" Every time I hear it, I think I'm supposed to put my breast in an envelope and send it to someone.

JAN KING

The play was a great success, but the audience was a disaster.

OSCAR WILDE

Nihilistic Knock Knock Joke:

Knock knock.

Who's there?

No one.

All images © Getty Images unless stated

Title page, Stan Laurel and Oliver Hardy, circa 1928
p.8, Lads having a laugh, circa 1955
p.11, Man pulling a funny face, circa 1920
p.14, Jerry Lewis in The Nutty Professor, 1963
p.18–19, Bathers at Chiswick, 1926
p.20, Young girl with pigtails laughing, 1955
p.24–25, Elderly woman laughing, 1976
p.26–27, Laughing competition, 1933
p.29, A pantomime horse, St. Moritz, circa 1935
p.32–33, Members of Lester's Midgets take a break from their show in London, 1964
p.34–35, People playing in the snow, 1978
p.37, Norman Wisdom performing, 1958
p.38–39, An elderly farmer smiling, circa 1945
p.41, A black spaghetti straw hat, a summer fashion from Italy, 1954
p.42, Stan Laurel and Oliver Hardy, circa 1930
p.44–45, A woman pulling her friend's foot, 1938
p.46, The Formakin Animal Training School, Oxfordshire, UK, 1962
p.50–51, Nick Stuart and Sally Phipps in a scene from News Parade, 1928
p.52–53, French film actress Mila Parely, 1947
p.55, The most perfect robot in the world, 1932
p.56–57, A musician relaxes in the shade of his instrument, Miami University, Florida, 1966
p.59, Bruce Lacy, nicknamed the "Mad Professor" at his home in London, 1962
p.60–1, A boy looking at a sign on the beach, 1934
p.63, Harry Secombe pulling a face, 1965
p.64–65, A baby in a toy car with a pet dog, 1935
p.67, A poodle puppy with its parent, 1955
p.68, Richard Arlen and Mary Brian filming The Light of the Western Stars, circa 1930
p.70–71, Children with fireworks, 1934
p.72–73, A dog at the wheel of a car, circa 1930
p.75, Pantomime donkey costume, London, 1938
p.78–79, Babies in a metal washtub, circa 1945
p.80–81, Agricultural show, Hertfordshire, UK, 1936
p.82–83, Rehearsals for a performance of Robinson Crusoe in London, 1936
p.85, Jackie Coogan as Uncle Fester from the TV series, The Addams Family, circa 1965
p.88–89, Two loving piglets, 1969
p.90–91, Dick Emery wearing cat's whiskers and a furry suit awaiting take-off clearance, 1963
p.94–95, Captain Birds Eye, fictional figurehead of the frozen food company Birds Eye, circa 1980
p.96–97, A man stares at a naturist, 1959
p.98–99, Federico Fellini and his wife, circa 1955
p.102–103, Sea-ranger Girl Guides, 1948
p.104, A member of the Sheffield Amalgamated Anglers Society, UK, 1949
p.109, An actor in the play, Master of Arts, 1949

p.110, An animal trainer at the Miami Seaquarium, circa 1977

p.112–113, The Amphicar which can be driven on land or water, 1964

p.116–117, Paul Chicago walking on the waters of the Chicago River, circa 1933

p.119, Two flappers on a beach, circa 1928

p.122–123, Fishwives, Great Yarmouth, UK, 1936

p.124–125, Ozzie and Harriet Nelson with their sons in *Here Come the Nelsons*, 1951

p.126–127, Butlin's holiday camp, UK, 1953

p.128–129, A man dozing, Hyde Park, London, 1952

p.132, A boy with water from a watering-can running down his face, 1962

p.135, A baby, 1945 © Lambert/Getty Images

p.139, Boy sticking his tongue out, circa 1955 © Lambert/Getty Images

p.142–143, A jogger on a Jersey beach, 1953

p.146, Arthur Askey dressed as an old woman in the film *Charley's Big-Hearted Aunt*, 1940

p.148–149, Phil Silvers playing cards with Tommy Trinder at London Airport, 1959

p.152–153, A camping holiday, 1936

p.155, A little girl dousing her dad, 1936

p.156–157, A carrot shaped like a hand, 1970

p.159, A man eating a hero sandwich, 1965

p.160–161, A man carries a stuffed bear, 1937

p.164, A boy holding a 2-foot cucumber, 1940

p.166–167, Comedian entertaining a crowd outdoors, circa 1955

p.168, Three teenage boys bite into the same hero sandwich, circa 1945

p.170–171, A pet goose with his mistress, 1936

p.173, Two boys eating large pieces of watermelon, circa 1955

p.176, An expression of disgust, circa 1955

p.179, Adam West and Burt Ward as Batman and Robin, with Sammy Davis Jnr., 1966

p.180–181, A shared joke in a bar, 1957

p.182–183, A child crying with a bowl of spaghetti tipped over its head, 1967

p.186–187, A "bicycle for four," circa 1935

p.189, The Cybermen, characters from British TV drama, *Dr. Who*, 1967

p.190–191, A house being transported on a trailer along a road in Nevada, USA, 1960

p.192–193, A dispatch rider makes a spectacular leap over two ponies, 1939

p.196–197, Buster Keaton and Fatty Arbuckle, 1918

p.199, Harry Langdon in *Heart Trouble*, 1928

p.200–201, A drunken owner "parked" his car in a swimming pool in Beverly Hills, 1961

p.205, A man makes a funny face, circa 1955

p.206–207, DM Copley is given a helping hand in this 1898 Renault at a hill climb

p.209, Rodney Twitchett, 1942

p.210–211, A couple on bicycle boats, 1925

p.212–213, A "Velocar" with "double-pedal" movement helps petrol rationing in London, 1939

p.214–215, Chris Marrion boards a bus with a stuffed crocodile under his arm, 1974

p.216–217, Three Windmill Theatre dancers on the beach at Angmering, UK, 1952